THE LIFE OF A
TEENAGE GIRL

ILLUSTRATED BY
Samantha Bright

AMYA MEEKINS

ISBN: 9781096634843
Library of Congress Catalog Number:

Cover Art By: Write on Promotions
Copyediting By: Keyoka Kinzy
Illustrator: Samantha Bright
Cover and Typeset Layout: Write on Promotions
Typeset By: Write on Promotions

To my fellow Gen Zers,

This book was written to help you find your inner worth and introduce you to self-love. It's important to love yourself first, you'll love others better. This book will also help you find your inner light and teach you how to use your God-given voice to be the change we want to see in our futures. We're equal in the eyes of God, no matter what society states. The color of your skin doesn't define you. You're great because He said so and He created you. Use your gifts to make a change. No matter your race or gender, YOU MATTER. YOUR VOICE MATTERS. OUR FUTURES MATTER. Be a CHANGEMAKER.

Dedication:

Thank you, God, for giving me the opportunity to have a chance to write this book. Your will be done. I pray that this book changes and empowers youth across the world. Thank you to my mother for being supportive of me no matter what. You pushed me to continue this book through all of its hardships and I'm thankful. Thank you to my supportive peers. You guys are awesome and rock!

The Life of a Teenage Girl

Chapter One:

I couldn't believe the words that had just come out of his mouth...

In my head, I didn't know if I should flip out or just burst into tears. Honestly, I felt like doing both. I heard my big brother's voice echoing in my head: "Never let them see you sweat." Unfortunately, that's hard to do right now. It felt like there was "embarrassment juice" flowing through my veins replacing the blood. How could something I couldn't change about myself be so powerful? I was in the middle of the hallway and there were a bunch of kids crowded around me in a circle. Some shook, some thought it was hilarious, and some just continued doing what they were doing before the incident occurred. The incident that would change my life forever; I just didn't know it yet.

Faith Tia Brown. Yeah, that's what my parents named me. I'm sixteen years old and I attend Westrock High School in Westrock. I was raised in Westrock for sure, but I learned a place couldn't define me as a person. Now, when most

Amya Meekins

people think of Westrock, they think of two things: talent and high crime. We have a lot of talent that comes from Westrock, from athletes to singers to rappers. Yeah, y'all know that rapper, Young Rich. Well, he's from right here. He was actually a close friend of mine, but we lost contact. I haven't seen him since he came back to do a toy drive for Christmas a few years back. For Trevor, A.K.A "Young Rich," to be seventeen, he's stupid rich. His grandma still stays in Westrock though. Ms. Grace doesn't plan on leaving either. Every time I visit after school, she always tells me the only way she's leaving is if the Lord's coming back. I love Ms. Grace. She's so sweet. She just wishes her grandson, Trevor, would stop living that lifestyle, especially in the public eye.

By the way, another talented person, Ryan Richardson, one of our high school basketball stars. He's so cute. He's super tall with smooth, even-toned brown skin, beady eyes, and he has a low fade cut with a part in it, like Nas, the rapper. We used to be friends in Kindergarten, but we don't even talk now. He's popular in our high school and I'm just me. Growing up in Westrock is hard. Your kind of forced to grow up fast, especially our young boys. Here in Westrock, everyone knows everyone. At Westrock High, it's popular to get pregnant, do drugs, and pretend. Due to the amount of violence and poverty in the area, most of us have to take on responsibilities that other kids our age may not have to face, but it isn't all bad. It's just how we were raised. Every day, we survive so much. Our environment is not the prettiest sight to look at. There's a group of young men on every corner as you past by the streets. You got their OG passing by all the blocks to make sure their handling their business the way their supposed to. You see some little kids at the park entrance trying to make some money to purchase themselves some new kicks by selling waters and water ice. By every corner store, you see a person without a home hustling to try to make ends meet. One thing about Westrock is this city is full of hustlers. I don't feel like people commit these actions of hustling because they want to. I feel like it's more that they have to do them to survive. Drugs, murders, and etc. are all these people know, which is sad.

If I had the tools and the outlets to make a change, Lord knows I would. From time to time, we'll have people throw events and complete their service hours, but nobody really tries to attach themselves to our community to make a real change. People are so worried about their "image" and not really helping to save lives. Sometimes, people fake like their hashtag

Amya Meekins

"woke", but that's just "for the 'gram.'" All the people here need is some hope, to feel some encouragement. I'll never forget when Trevor came and did that toy drive for Christmas. The whole community was out together. No violence, and you could feel the love.

Ring! Ring! The school bell rang loud, echoing in the hallways. There was lots of commotion, sneakers screeching down the hallways, lockers being slammed. The hallways were a bit stuffy from all the activity throughout the day, so it was a bit smelly. It smelt like gym socks and pure sweat.

"Aww man," I said.

"What's up girl?" I heard my bestest friend in the whole wide world, Aya, say. I turned around. Aya is so pretty. She's tall with medium-brown skin, big, beautiful brown eyes, and her jumbo box braids sat on her head in a bun with her baby hairs slayed to the gods. How were her baby hairs still laid after a long, stuffy day in school? She had to have used that EcoStyler Gel I put her into. That stuff works magic!

"Nothing much, girl, I was just a little irritated. you know, it's pouring outside and my hair!" I explained to my friend.

Today, I had my natural hair out in an afro. It was moisturized well and curly. Since I had a lot of hair, I didn't even want to deal with having to put it in a ponytail.

"Girl, now you know you've got good hair, c'mon now," Aya said.

"Aya, chill! All hair is beautiful," I told her.

"Yeah, girl, whatever," Aya stated, rolling her eyes. "Are you riding the bus today?" "Nah, sis, I'm going to walk," I answered.

"If you are walking, why are you fussing about your hair then?" she asked. In my head, I definitely rolled my eyes. Aya can be a piece of work sometimes, I tell you, but she's my girl, so I deal with her.

"Aya, I would have to walk regardless, duh, home from the bus stop. Plus, I want to stop by Ms. Grace's house before I head home."

"Ooooooo, girl, you just want to get the latest tea on Trevor. You know, I was scrolling on Instagram yesterday, and I see that him and that reality TV star, Kye Rose, broke up."

"Dang, girl, that's a mess," I said. Aya was right. I did have a crush on Trevor just a little bit, but I wasn't telling her that. If I told Aya, she would never let the situation die down, ESPECIALLY if we saw Trevor. Oh my gosh, Lord knows I can see it now.

Click! The doors opened and school was over. Teenagers were being loud everywhere.

Amya Meekins

TextSnap videos were being made. There was play-fighting from the boys, girls tried to start some drama, and other girls were in the guys' faces while waiting for the bus to arrive, so we all could go home. Shaking my head...that's Westrock High School for ya. By now, the rain had stopped. It was still wet outside, but the sun is shining, which created rainbows on the school's sidewalks and concrete.

"Ay, Faith, you see Denise? She's never going to learn," said Aya.

"Aya, girl, mind your business. I don't want no drama with Denise," I said.

Aya blabbered on and on about Denise and her latest drama in front of me, but I was too busy focused on Denise in Ryan Richardson's face. He was feeling her, too. She put her arm on his shoulder and everything. Ryan's clique surrounded them, "his boys," all basketball players. They had on their dark green and gray varsity basketball jackets with their last names and numbers on the back.

When I was little, I always thought I would have a relationship like Gabriella and Troy from *High School Musical. I could* rock my high school sweetheart's jacket, but *sheesh*! Life had other plans for me, I guess. Ryan interrupted my thoughts. He looked up at me as Denise whispered something in his ear. Man, oh man, all I saw was his waves spinning for sure. He definitely just went to the barbershop because his hairline was crisp. The diamond studs in his ear glistened as the sun shined through them.

I guess Denise felt him not paying her attention anymore because she stopped and turned her head to look at what he was looking at. When she saw it was me, she sucked her teeth hard. Denise was very popular. Her skin complexion was lighter than mine. She favored the girls you would see on the "Explore" page on Instagram. Yeah, she's that type of pretty. Her eyebrows were bomb, and she kept her face beat. She had her Brazilian inches hanging down her back too. She removed her arm from around Ryan's neck, folded them across her chest, and looked at me. That's when I knew there was about to be war with her.

When I got dressed for school this morning, my all-white Air Force Ones looked extra "crispy," but now, as I walk home, I'm kind of annoyed I chose to wear these and it rained. I don't play about my hair or my kicks. I don't need any mud ruining my shoes. Plus, my Momma would kill me. As I walked home, Lil' Baby blasted through my Air Pods and my curls bounced up and down; some stuck to my lip gloss. Ugh, I truly hated when that happened. That's like every girl's nightmare. I was so into

Amya Meekins

my music; I hadn't noticed that I had reached Ms. Grace's house. She was outside on her porch, making sure her plants looked nice. I loved her like my Grandma. Ms. Grace is an older lady with such a wise soul. She's about my height, or even shorter than me, actually. Her skin is smooth and dark brown, like a Hershey bar.

In the front of her house, I could see that her big, bright red tomatoes were ready to be cooked for some delightful spaghetti. That lady sure knows she can cook! I tried to come by to check on her since Trevor wasn't always around or able to anymore. Trevor's mom is his manager with a few other major artists. She's always fussing and says she doesn't have the time to see about her mother, but that's crap because even Trevor, the artist, finds time.

"Aww, my baby, Faith, how are you doing today, dear?" Ms. Grace greeted me.

"I'm fine, Ms. Grace. How are you doing?"

"I'm fine, baby. God woke me up this morning, so I must be onto something here."

I chuckled, "I hear you, Ms. Grace. Well, I was just stopping by. Momma needs me home in time for dinner tonight. She has some errands to do."

"Oh wow, your Momma's cooking? That poor baby. Here, I'll put some of my fresh spaghetti in a container for you two."

"Aw Ms. Grace, that's so nice of you. I'm sure Momma will be happy, and I know she'll appreciate it for sure."

Well, looks like Zay, my brother, Isaiah, is going to be hungry tonight, I thought to myself. I know for sure my Momma isn't cooking anything at all now. Knowing Zay though, he'll get one of his little girlfriends to bring him some food. My brother is a mess. He's brown skin, about six feet and two inches tall, and has hazel eyes. He gets his looks from our Daddy, but you can tell my Momma smoothed him out. My brother's handsome. He taught me about the shoe game too. He makes sure we're fresh, just like my Momma. He used to attend Westrock High and played for our basketball team, but he graduated. He still sometimes goes around to help coach the team though.

As I came out of my thoughts, I heard Ms. Grace's screen door crack open. She came outside with two large containers of spaghetti. She even had the garlic bread wrapped up in foil on the top.

"Aw, Ms. Grace, you're so sweet to us. Thank you so much," I said.

9

Amya Meekins

"No problem, baby, and remember to tell your Nana to call me back. We never got to Macy's."

"Okay, I got you. See you later. Stay safe."

"Alright baby, you too," she said. She watched me walk down the steps off her porch and down the street.

"Stay safe" was something everyone said in Westrock. It's not because we want to, but it's because we have too. Bullets here have no name on them.

When I got home, I could hear the TV, so that meant my brother was playing video games, per usual. After I opened the door, I went straight to the kitchen and put the food on the table.

"Hey, big head," stated Isaiah when he heard me come in.

"Hey, ugly," I replied.

"How was school?" he asked.

"Nothing really, per usual. You know, Sean asked about you."

"Yeah, he texted me. We going to go to the courts Friday to play a game with the boys." "Oh, and Alex asked about you too...which is weird because she doesn't even talk to me," I said, making sure to loudly suck my teeth and roll my eyes. "Man...she better go ahead somewhere," said Zay, twisting a piece of his hair. He laid back on the couch and put his arm up. Alex is my brother's ex-girlfriend of three years. She's just weird to me. She never really talked to me before or after their relationship, but every time she wants a message passed to him, all of a sudden, she knows who I am. I cannot do the weirdness. I had too much going on right now to be worried about iffy people.

I went to the kitchen to heat up my container of spaghetti from Ms. Grace's house. Once my food was done, I got a cold glass of lemonade and sat down to eat and do homework. As I finished up some Algebra II work, my brother walked into the kitchen and just stared at me.

"Yes, Zay, may I help you?" I asked, staring back.

"Um...where is my food?" He pulled his neck back, furrowed his eyebrows, and made his lip go up.

"Oh, my bad. I stopped by Ms. Grace's house before I came here. Momma was supposed to cook, but you know she isn't now. Just make you something or order something to eat."

"Faith...that's not the point. That spaghetti smells mad good. What makes you think I don't want any?"

"Zay, I know you want some, but the thing is...you're not getting any."

Amya Meekins

Zay just looked at me with his head tilted sideways for a moment. Then, he sucked his teeth and walked out the kitchen.

"Finally," I yelled and took a deep breath as I finished my homework. I put the pieces of paper back into a folder and placed the folder into my backpack. I headed upstairs to get ready for bed. It just felt like tomorrow was going to be a long day.

Chapter Two:

"Hey, honey," my Momma said as I came down the stairs and into the kitchen. I could smell the scrambled eggs and bacon cooking on the stove.

"Hey, Mommy, how'd you sleep?"

"Well, I slept pretty well. How about you?"

"Good. Can I take some food with me as I walk to school?" I asked her.

"Yes, of course, you want to take some for Aya as well?" My Momma asked.

"Eh, let me text her and ask."

"Okay, and baby have a great day today," she said.

"Okay..." I looked at her strangely. My Momma always wanted me to have a great day and she always said it, but something about today just felt totally different.

Aya and I walked through those double doors and immediately, I knew something was off. Students would stare at me in their little cliques, then turn back to themselves and laugh.

Amya Meekins

"Aya, what's wrong with everybody?" I asked. I held my backpack straps and turned around to see everyone.

"Girl, I don't know, but they need to watch it," she answered. Everything was so strange. Aya and I walked down the hallway to our lockers. They were side by side.

"Okay, girl, I'm getting sick of this. What the heck is going on?" Aya asked, slamming her locker. She rolled her eyes and her neck as she examined the hallway.

"I don't know," I told her. I put my combination in the locker and grabbed my American Government textbook. That's when I heard the snickering behind me. I threw my hoodie into my locker and the snickering grew louder. I closed my locker and put my American government textbook up to my chest with both hands. I turned around to see what the snickering was about and who was laughing. I saw Ryan Richardson and his boys in my peripheral vision. Ryan looked at me and smirked. I was so confused. I looked at Aya for an answer and she shrugged her shoulders.

Next thing you know, my phone lit up. There was a Text Snap from someone mentioning me in their story. I clicked on the notification to open it, and it felt like my heart dropped down to my knees. I was instantly heartbroken. I just didn't know how to feel. I never felt this way before nor have I ever experienced this before. Aya looked at me and saw that I wasn't 100% fine. She peeped over my shoulder to see what I was looking at. Her mouth flew open. It was just so devastating...

Someone had screenshotted a picture of Ryan's private TextSnap story. He had posted a picture of my face photoshopped onto the body of a monkey with the words, "Dark Monkey," as the caption. I was so confused. I couldn't believe Ryan would do something like that. I was so lost for words that I couldn't even react.

"Ryan, you're sick!" Aya snapped. "What is wrong with you? What did Faith ever do to you to make you humiliate her on this level? You should be absolutely ashamed of yourself. My friend isn't a 'dark monkey.' She's a queen. You should feel real dumb talking about someone of your own race like that. We don't exploit our own people, Ryan!"

"Well...your friend shouldn't look like a burnt French fry," Ryan said.

I was so struck by how he had humiliated me in front of most of the school. At Westrock High, things traveled extra fast. I was sure the rest of the school was aware of what was going on.

15

Amya Meekins

"WHAT DID YOU SAY?" Aya screamed. She was ready to jump across the hallway at Ryan. "What do you mean 'burnt French fry,' Ryan?"

"Her skin tone...it's dark. She's black as asphalt. If we were to turn all of these lights out right now, you would not see her," he yelled back.

All I could do was stare at him. I didn't know how to react. I hadn't heard those things about myself before. Was this what my ancestors had gone through? Is this what it feels like to be a Black girl? Why? I had so many questions. I was heartbroken. It felt like my heart had hit the floor and shattered into a million and one pieces.

Ryan and I used to be friends when we were younger and I had a little crush on him too, so hearing those words from him hurt even more. He wasn't even that much lighter than me. I was just confused by why he thought it was okay to pick on his own race. All of society did it anyway. My Momma always told me I was beautiful. She made sure to instill that in me while I was young. It hurt so much that I didn't want anyone else to feel this pain. Why did being darker matter so much to people? Why can't we all just be beautiful in our own way?

I sat at my desk in the middle of the classroom. Our teacher was teaching us conversion factors in chemistry class. I should've really been paying attention, but I just couldn't focus since that incident occurred. I literally felt like I was just existing. Mentally, I wasn't there. I had never dealt with that level of embarrassment before and just didn't know what to do.

Ring ring! Just like that, school was done for the day. I threw my backpack around my shoulders, holding my textbook up to my chest as I walked out. My mind was all over the place, but hey, could you blame me? What Ryan had said about me was honestly sickening. I headed to my locker to put up my textbook and grab my hoodie to walk home. That's when this girl came up to me.

"Hey, Faith, I heard about what happened with Ryan. I'm really sorry that happened to you," she said. "We've never interacted before, but I've seen you around school. You seem like you have such a sweet, genuine soul. Keep being great, girl! Don't let that tear you down." she smiled at me.

I literally had never seen her before, but what she said to me was so kind. God always has a way of doing things. I really needed that.

Amya Meekins

"Wow...thank you. That was sweet of you," I said, looking down then back up at her. "I really needed to hear that, so thanks a lot."

"No problem, girl! You never know; things always happen for a reason. Maybe this can benefit you in the future."

"Well, girl, I sure hope you're right. I'll see you around," I said, closing my locker. With a final wave to her, I headed home. As I walked home, I fell deeper and deeper into my thoughts. The incident continued to replay in my mind over and over again. That photo of me kept popping up in my head too. I was so hurt. Before I knew it, I was at Ms. Grace's house. Right then and there, I knew God definitely had a reason for things.

Chapter Three:

Ms. Grace was usually home at this time, so I walked up onto her porch and knocked on her door. She didn't answer. I knocked a few more times, then looked into her backyard. *Boo yah!* I jogged down her porch steps and pushed open the gate. Ms. Grace was on her hands and knees, patting down soil. There were various fruits and vegetables being grown in Ms. Grace's garden. No wonder her food was so mouthwatering; it's organic. "Hello, Miss. Lady!" I called. She turned around to see me and smiled a bit. She pulled her arm out and motioned for me to come over. I walked over to where she was and sat down at the table beside her.

"Hey dear, what makes you stop by? How was school today?" Ms. Grace asked.

"Well, Ms. Grace, I know for a fact I can't lie to you without you knowing, so I might as well tell you the whole truth and nothing but the truth," I said.

Amya Meekins

Ms. Grace stopped what she was doing and turned around fully. She stood up, dusted her hands off, and took off her gloves. She pulled out a chair, placed the gloves on the table, and sat down with a worried look on her face.

"Spill," she said.

"So, today I experienced my first brush with colorism...through cyber bullying."

"Oh, my goodness," Ms. Grace said. She always said "goodness" instead of using God's name in vain.

"Yeah, Ms. Grace, when I was at school, I got a notification on my phone from an old friend. He had photoshopped my picture onto the body of a monkey. Then, he called me names. I'm not going to lie; I stayed very strong throughout the day, but honestly, it hurt my heart to the core. My skin color isn't something I'd ever thought I would have a problem with at school, especially not with another black person. Maybe if I was at the store and an incident occurred, like you hear on television, but not...not by another black person. This feeling is something I wouldn't want anybody to have to feel."

"Baby let me tell you a story that happened to my Momma when she was about your age," Ms. Grace said. "One day, my mom and a group of her friends were hungry after school. They wanted to get a bite to eat at this restaurant called Tony's in downtown Westrock. As I'm sure you're aware of now, that restaurant is no longer open. A Caucasian man owned the place, but he had African American cooks and workers. My mom and her friends came in there chatting with one another about their crushes at school. They opened the door, too intrigued by their conversation to notice anything odd and sat at the bar, waiting to be served. That's when the owner, Tony, approached them with a paper bag in his hand."

"A paper bag, Ms. Grace? What did he plan to do with it?" I asked her.

"Faith, a paper bag had a lot of power back in those days, but back to the story. So, Tony approached the girls and said, 'I'm sorry, but if you're darker than this paper bag, I will have to ask you to leave. We will not serve you here. You're not permitted.'"

"Are you serious?" I asked in disbelief.

"Yep! That's what happened. My momma was worried because she knew she was way darker than that paper bag. One of her friends was pushing it and others were okay, but not her. Once Tony had gotten to my mom, he looked at her sternly and stated, 'Young lady,

Amya Meekins

I'm going to have to ask you to go. You do not meet the serving requirements here. Please leave. If you do not leave, I will call the police.'"

"Wow, Ms. Grace, why did he have to take it that far? He could've just served her," I said.

"Well, baby, things weren't like that back then; it wasn't as easy as it is now. They both could have gotten into some serious trouble or even killed."

"That's just so sad. It really is. In God's eyes, we're all equal. I wish it would be the same on Earth," I said.

"Me too, honey. Prayerfully, I'll live to see the day that happens. Maybe you can help fight and make the change we want to see," said Ms. Grace.

"Eh, maybe, Ms. Grace, but I don't know if I could do all of that."

"Hey hey hey! I hope what happened to you isn't starting to dim your confidence, honey," she exclaimed. "Oh no! Ms. Grace doesn't play that now. Honey, you take what that boy said to you, and you use it to make you better. You're beautiful and deep down you know it too. You're a sweet girl. If that little boy doesn't recognize that, then something is wrong with him. I hate that that even happened to you." Ms. Grace rolled her eyes, clearly upset.

She was so flustered and mad. "Hey, how about we enjoy some brownies? Just me and you."

"Can we add some butter pecan ice cream?" I asked.

"You know it."

We started for the house, walking side by side. Ms. Grace put her hand on my back for emotional support. I didn't mind it at all; it was just what I needed.

Chapter Four:

When I arrived back at school the next day, it wasn't as awkward as I thought it'd be. Everyone still glanced at me from time to time when I walked down the halls. Aya wasn't there and wouldn't be for the next few days, so it kind of sucked. She was the only person I really kicked it with. She had to get her wisdom teeth pulled out. Whew...lucky her. Ugh! It sucked to even say that. As I walked to my next class from my locker, I saw this girl looking the exact same way I looked yesterday. I could see straight through the gimmicks. She was hurting, and I knew how she felt. I knew the Lord was working on me for sure. Before the incident with Ryan, Lord knows, I wouldn't have said or done anything just because of who she was. She was Denise. ...

Yes, the pretty girl who was just yesterday all in Ryan Richardson's face. Well, honey, the script had most definitely flipped. Now, he and his friends were being colorist to Denise. Yesterday, it was me for being dark skinned;

today, it's her for being light skinned. What is wrong with them? And it's funny because Ryan's complexion is literally in between the both of ours. I know his preference is for girls who are Puerto Rican with curly hair, but that doesn't mean he has to talk down on women in his own race. Denise was posted up with her back on the locker. Ryan had his arm around her, and his friends were crowded around them both. As Ryan put on his clownery show, Denise put her head down and kept tucking her hair behind her ear. She saw me looking at her through the boys standing in front of her. They were all too busy running their mouths to even notice the conversation she and I were having with our eyes. Ryan saw where Denise was looking, but I turned my head quickly, looking down before he noticed me. I walked passed them, but Denise still stared at me. It felt weird. It was like he had control over me. Since when was I fearful of what somebody thought of me? Since when did I ever question the way God made me?

Chapter Five:

I was in my room, chilling on my bed, scrolling through Twitter, when I came across a tweet about colorism. Someone had tweeted, "Y'all dark skin girls gonna bathe this year or nah?" Ew. How can you be so rude and not even use the correct spelling or grammar? That was like the second rude post on social media about skin complexion that I had seen that night. For some reason, seeing posts like that just struck me to the core. Everything Ryan said that day in school replayed in my head. I could remember every detail of that photoshopped picture. It was hard to get rid of.

The torment had to stop. It was not cool at all. There must be a way to stop thinking about that incident and torturing myself about it. I don't think anyone should have to go through something like that. If I don't end it, at least I can fight against it in a way. I know that as long as somebody's life is changed by me using my voice, I'm cool. As a victim of bullying, I felt it was necessary for all skin complexions to be represented and know that they're beautiful.

I'm just trying to find ways to stop the colorism amongst us. We need to all practice self-confidence when we wake up in the morning. Colorism is something that divides us into groups, but we need to come together to stop it. People don't think light skinned people get bullied for their skin complexion, but as I saw earlier, it happened to Denise. I could start a movement to stop it, but how can I start a movement?

As I sat on my bed, I got a tag on Instagram from somebody who goes to my school. Before I could open it, I received a text message from Aya. *Ugh, isn't she supposed to be resting, I thought? I guess* she was stuck in bed and didn't have much else to do. So, I clicked on Aya's text message.

Aya: Girl I'm about sick n TIRED of them kids at school

Me: ??

Aya: There's a video of Ryan Richardson making fun of you going viral.

Me: R U Serious?

Aya: YES! *face palm emoji*

I literally dropped the phone in my lap and breathed out loudly. I'm so tired of this. The

Amya Meekins

worst part is that Ryan is the last person I would ever expect to do something like this to me.

Chapter Six:

Ugh! I yawned, waking up. I didn't even remember falling asleep the night before. That stuff bugged me out for real. I even had a dream that Trevor contacted me again, which is weird. It's Saturday, so I'm off from school, and honestly, your girl isn't tripping. I could really use the break from all the academic work and social stress, you know? I went into the bathroom and did my morning hygiene, then headed downstairs to get some breakfast. Zay was at the kitchen table, munching on some pancakes, scrambled eggs with cheese, and applewood bacon.

"Hey, little sis!" he said when he saw me. "Mom ran out for her hair appointment and said she'll be back by lunchtime. I left you some breakfast on the stove,"

Now, that was very kind of my brother. Yeah, he is a boy and boys eat a lot, but it was nice of him to leave me some food. Although I didn't share my food with him the other day, here he was leaving some breakfast for me. I expected him to pay me back the next opportunity he got, but shoot, I'm not tripping.

"Aw thanks, Zay! That was mad nice of you," I said with a grin.

The food was still hot. I piled up heaps, stopping to cut up a few strawberries, and sat down to eat. I said grace, took my vitamins, and ate while scrolling through my Instagram timeline. The video of Ryan and I was on another blog, a major one. It had over a thousand comments and counting. Aya was absolutely right. It was a video of Ryan disrespecting me in the hallway with someone recording and laughing. You could see people surrounding us.

Zay looked at my face, clearly, he had heard what Ryan had said to me. Lots of people were in the comments defending Ryan. Some were harsh, but some people were in between.

"Ay! I'm sorry that happened to you, Faith," Zay said. "I'll check Ryan my dang own self. You don't have to worry about anything at all. He got me messed up, thinking he can mess with my flesh and blood."

"No Zay, just leave it. Don't hurt him," I told my brother.

"Don't hurt him? Girl what?! You are tripping for real. You need to get on that internet and defend yourself as soon as possible," he said.

Zay was right. I should defend myself. Later on, I set my phone up on my vanity to get the right angle with the lights bright on my face. I fluffed out my hair to make sure it looked semi-neat. People were already on the internet bashing me, and I didn't need them talking about anything else, especially my hair. I don't play about my hair.

When I started the video, the words coming out of my mouth felt dumb. I talked and talked, but none of it felt real. I took a loud, deep breath and waited until I felt something deep down in me say: Start the video and let the words flow through you. So, I shook off the shame and started the video. As I talked, I realized how passionate I was about the issue. I went on and on. I ended the video off with "#MelaninMatters." It felt like a whole load was taken off of me, no lie. I sat there and rewatched the video before posting it. I made sure to tag #MelaninMatters in the description. With that done, I propped on my bed and turned to Netflix. I didn't have anything to do today, so I just wanted to binge-watch a series I had been meaning to get to, but I never had time to during the week.

Oh wow... I guess I had fallen asleep while watching TV. I picked up my phone and looked to see what time it was. There were tons of

31

notifications. This was the most my phone had ever popped. *What's going on?!* I wondered. I went straight to Instagram. My mentions were going nuts! This one particular tag stuck out to me more than the others because it was Trevor. Yep! My childhood crush had posted the video of me speaking about colorism.

My mouth was wide-open. I hadn't seen or talked to him in a while. I was thankful he posted the video to defend me. Trevor had 6.5 million followers on Instagram, and somehow, he saw what I was doing and cared. That honestly meant a lot to me.

I read the caption: *Faith is my friend and to see her highlighted in the blogs this way hurts me. Baby girl, you know, I'm always there for you. You know, you're beautiful and deep down that jerk does too. All shades of melanin is beautiful. #MelaninMatters All skin tones should be represented, so colorism can be stopped. Faith, we're turtle pals forever. Whenever you see this, call me.*

I couldn't help but blush after reading Trevor's heartfelt message. *Ugh! Faith you need to stop crushing on your friend.* I thought. I scrolled down to the comments. Girls left messages with heart emojis and stuff like, "Aw, I wish Young Rich thought of me like that" and "That Faith girl is lucky." There were other comments that weren't the nicest, but it's cool. I slid my finger across the screen and saw that a blue check had left me a direct message. "I'm sorry about what happened to you," the message from Trevor said. "Facetime me when you're free.". I fell back onto my bed and felt my face heating up. He was all like "when you're free." Wasn't he the superstar, who's constantly busy, but he wants me to call him when I'm free? So sweet. I marked a mental note to call him. When I went to the post on my actual page, there were many blue checks who left me comments. Who knew something so little in my head could be so much bigger, but little did I know, God had way bigger plans.

Chapter Seven:

I was playing *Slices* on my phone when a notification popped up that I had received a direct message on Instagram. My favorite actress and activist, Angelina Thomas, had left me a heartfelt message. Oh, my goodness! This was too much.

In her message, Angelina talked about how she sometimes felt colorism in the film industry. There was a big deal about what the leading roles looked like, and she thought on-screen love interests should show all races and all shades of people. She told me how proud she was of me, which meant a lot because she's somebody I look up to. She said she tries to use her voice for human rights and loves how I used my voice to speak on such a touchy subject. She said she was sorry that that situation occurred, but she knows bigger things are ahead for me! She told me to keep God first and continue to do great things in my generation. Also, she said she posted my video because more people need to hear what I have to say.

The last thing she said to me, and this part almost made me fall on the floor and literally scream so loud, was that she called in a favor to one of her good friends, Robin Kinnis. Robin Kinnis was a major talk show host, who wanted to bring me on her show to talk about what happened to me. If I went on that show, I knew I could spread my hashtag, MelaninMatters even more. Even now, it's trending on Twitter. My video went viral overnight, so it's now a movement. So many people were speaking out about how they felt and it's really heartwarming to see all people coming together for something like this. I never really thought this would go this far.

I heard a knock on my door. It was my Momma with a bowl of chocolate-covered strawberries. My favorite.

"You busy?" my Mom asked.

"Nope, I'm just chilling, Momma. You can come in."

My Momma sat in the chair in front of my vanity. She placed the bowl of strawberries on my bed and grabbed one to chew on.

"So, baby," she said, "I saw your video on Facebook."

No lie, when she said that, I started feeling butterflies in my stomach. I didn't know how she was going to react to the whole situation. So, I

Amya Meekins

waited to see what she was going to say because honestly, I was very nervous.

"I just wanted to let you know that I'm very proud of you for standing up for that cause," she said. "I'm sorry I haven't been that active in your life lately, but just know that I'm so proud of you. A lot of people were sharing it online and talking about how brave, beautiful, and strong you are, baby."

"Aw, thank you, Mom," I told her. "I'm sorry I didn't bring it to your attention, but I didn't know how serious it was until I saw the reaction from the video. Guess what, though?"

"What's up?"

"Angelina Thomas reached out to me. She wants me to go on Robin Kinnis' talk show. Mom, do you know how big that is? So many celebrities go on there to talk about stuff. So, for her to even invite me is huge, in my opinion, because I'm not a celebrity."

"Yes, baby, I do understand how huge it is. You will be in attendance, and well, honey, it looks like you're kind of are a celebrity now after all of this hectic stuff going on."

"Did you also see the actress, Heaven Green? She was talking about her experiences with colorism in the acting industry."

"Boo, I'm so proud of you. You have people across the world speaking about this. You're literally making a change. We have to do something with this #MelaninMatters because people are loving it."

As we talked, I was legit thinking about how I had listened to Ms. Grace and now, my life is changing. She was the one who told me that everything happened for a reason. It sucks that I had to go through some trauma to get here, but I don't regret it at all. People are gaining awareness about the effects of colorism. Some people don't even know that they are performing acts of colorism. Some people don't even know the difference between colorism and racism. As I was going deeper into my thoughts, I said a prayer to God:

Wow, God, you never seem to fail me. I love how you flipped what I was struggling with to be one of the best things to ever happen to me. You know, you keep raising me up to be strong. Thank you for using me for your work to be done, for changes to be made, for barriers to be broken, and for lives to be saved. I ask that you keep me on track and make sure I do everything you want me to do with this campaign, Melanin Matters. I ask all of that in Jesus' name, I pray. Amen. God, you are something else.

Chapter Eight:

My Mom and I were driving over to Ms. Grace's house. It had been awhile since we had seen or heard from her. Plus, my Momma wanted to talk to her about my Melanin Matters movement. As I looked at the streets of Westrock, we passed by my school. There are boys outside the gym entrance, using the open gym on the weekend. The weather felt so good today. The sun was cooking my melanin skin. I had slathered myself in baby oil, so I was looking greasy but moisturized and fine. The windows were down, so our hair was blowing in the wind. Momma blasted her favorite singer, Kelli Tyra's, latest single called "First Love," and the bass was kicking out the speakers. I'm more into rap music, but I can't lie, this song was definitely a bop.

My brother and I were raised up on good music. So, when my Momma plays a song and says, "What you know about this?" We always look at her with confused faces because she definitely put us on. I was just bopping my head to the music when I felt my phone vibrate in my lap. I had a text from Aya. *Omg! It's been awhile since I heard from her, I thought.* I honestly missed her. I quickly put in my passcode, so I could answer her. With a smile, I texted her back, "hey, best friend" with many cute emojis. As Aya and I chatted, just catching up, suddenly, my Momma hollers. She scared me so bad, I jumped and felt my heartbeat speed up.

"Ma!!" I yelled, frowning.

"Girl, I'm sorry, but they're playing my jam!" she shouted and turned up the radio. She started dancing, throwing her arms up in the air and shaking her hips. She had her lips poked out and everything, you could tell Momma was definitely feeling this song.

It was so funny because it was Trevor being played. His song, "Millions," was hot like fire right now. You couldn't even scroll down your timeline without seeing somebody either playing it or dancing to it. One way or another, you were going to hear it. It was in the top ten on all music charts. I kept glancing over at my Mom and just loving how happy she was. I started recording us together on TextSnap, lip syncing Trevor's song, and posted it.

Before I knew it, we were pulling into Ms. Grace's driveway. My Mom turned the car off, grabbed her purse, and jumped out. I grabbed my purse and jumped out too. She locked the car with the remote and it made that clicking noise, so you knew it was locked. She put the little key fob in her purse and walked up to Ms. Grace's front door. I followed behind her, scrolling through my phone while Mama rang the doorbell.

Through the door, I could smell a bunch of foods cooking and my stomach growled. I smelled some collard greens, yams, baked mac and cheese, and fried chicken. Now, I knew Ms. Grace didn't do all this cooking for nothing. Ms. Grace only made spreads like that when she had great company... great company like...

The front door swung open. Ms. Grace stood there, smiling with her apron on, her arms wide open for hugs as she welcomed us in. She gave me a hug and held onto me longer than she did my Mom. She patted my back, which was very comforting and kissed me on my forehead. "How are you, dear? How have you been holding up?" Ms. Grace asked.

"I've been fine," I replied. "It hit the media now, so it's a blessing and a curse. Everything happens for a reason, though, and I know God will get me through this because His will be done."

She looked at me and smiled big. "That's my girl." She grabbed me closer to her side, put her arm around my back, and walked us into the living room of the house. I could hear my omma chatting with somebody and that voice sounded very, very familiar.

I looked up and there he was Trevor, aka Young Rich. As soon as he looked up at me, our eyes connected. The connection was deeper than anything physical; it was spiritual and mental. He stood at least a foot over me because I'm very short. His beautiful, almond-shaped light brown eyes stared down into my soul. It honestly felt like everything was going in slow motion. It felt like we were the only people in the world at that moment. He had his haircut into a Brooklyn like my brother and his eyebrows had two slits in them. The diamonds in his earrings were huge! We weren't even outside, and they were glistening. I imagined I would be blind if the sun was there. His skin looked flawless, literally. He was glowing. I literally saw no pimples, no teenage acne, even thinking about appearing on his face at all.

My eyes lowered down to his lips. They were a nice size and definitely kissable. His teeth were perfect. I guess having those braces when we were younger definitely paid off for him. He

Amya Meekins

had a diamond grill in his mouth, literally making his smile look like a million dollars. As soon as I was about to study his outfit, he said my name. Man, oh man, it sounded so lovely coming out of his mouth, literally music to my ears. As he said it, I watched a smile form on his lips, showing that he genuinely was excited to see me. He embraced me in a hug. Being in his arms definitely felt good. There was security and a vibe was there. He looked down at me and it was like he felt something too. There was chemistry between us, and I thought I could lay in his arms forever, but too soon, we pulled away. He looked at me like I was the most beautiful girl in the world. *Hopefully, in his eyes, I am*, I chuckled to myself.

"Faith, oh my gosh, hi. It's so good to see you. It's been awhile. You look so beautiful!"

"Oh, thank you," I said. "It's good to see you too."

"And hey, punk, you thought I forgot about that call you were supposed to give me, huh.?" he asked and smiled with a raised eyebrow.

I was just smiling and blushing from ear to ear.

"No, I planned to call you," I said, pushing my hair behind my ear. "I know you're always busy. I just didn't expect to run into you so soon, that's for sure. So, how have you been? You look great!"

"Shoot, I've been living, just trying to stay focused and do something positive, trying to stay out of trouble," he replied, brushing his hand across his face. "I'm sure you are. Everything's been looking like it's going good for you. 'Millions' is doing well. I'm so proud of you, Trevor, seriously." I grabbed his arm and looked into his eyes, so he knew I was serious. I could see through his cool demeanor and knew he was going through a lot on the inside.

"Yeah, thank you. I appreciate it, so I was thinking, and I want you to be in the music video for the song. I was going to tell you when you called me, but you never did so..." he said, then shrugged his shoulders.

"I feel like you're going to hold that over my head for a minute," I said, chuckling.

"So, besides the incident that happened, what's been going on at school? Man, believe it or not, sometimes, I miss going to Westrock High."

"I guess I could see why. Westrock High isn't the best, but we do have things you can love and miss. I can't sit up here and bash you about missing school because I would too, honestly," I said.

Amya Meekins

For a moment, Trevor's face shifted. It looked like he knew something I didn't know. "Man, look," he said, "you're going to feel just like me soon enough."

I was so confused, and my face showed it. "Trevor, what are you talking about?" Man, look," Trevor explained, "between you and me, when your movement pops off, you're going to be running nonstop. You're going to have to be homeschooled like me. Our mothers and my grandma were already discussing it. My mom is about to push you like no other, and maybe even become your manager. We all know she puts in work before anything else, so career-wise, you have nothing to worry about.

Before I could ask Trevor anymore questions, all of the ladies came into the room to tell us to come eat. I could smell all of my favorites, from yams to collard greens. Food covered every surface in the dining room.

"Please excuse me," I said. "I'm going to wash my hands before breaking bread." As I walked away, I felt eyes on my back.

I closed the bathroom door behind me and looked into my reflection in the mirror. I took a deep breath and analyzed myself. Everything was happening so quickly, and I was becoming overwhelmed. I sat back and thought about how my whole life had changed from that incident in school. Everyone on social media knew what happened to me and who I was I thought about what happened, how it happened, where it happened, how it affected me and others. Some people may call me crazy, but I didn't want people to continuously bash Ryan. Yes, he exposed his preferences regarding women, but if they know better, they'd do better. I thought about what folks would say if I stopped going to school. I'm sure it would receive a lot of negative feedback.

Knock! Knock! I turned on the faucet and washed my hands quickly, then grabbed a paper towel to dry them. When I opened the door, it was Ms. Grace standing there.

"Hey dear, is everything okay?" she asked. "I could see a shift in your energy after you and Trevor finished talking."

When she said that, I looked her in her eyes and burst out into tears. My heart was so heavy. I had so much built up in me. I hadn't realized that I never fully dealt with the incident. I was trying to move onto the next level in my life without dealing with it. Ms. Grace just embraced me. It wasn't just physically; it was like she embraced me spiritually as well. When Ms. Grace hugged me, I felt like God was giving me a hug through her. I felt so comforted and supported.

"Faith, baby, I feel like God is telling me to tell you something," said Ms. Grace, looking up at me. "Before you elevate in life, you have to let go and let God. You have to give your wounds unto Him to heal."

Chapter Nine:

Before I knew it, I was on the Robin Kinnis Talk Show, talking about the Melanin Matters Movement. I stood along the side of the stage, getting a mic put on me. I was behind these big, tall, black curtains and I could hear the crowd of people reacting to what Robin Kinnis was saying. All of the laughing and clapping only made my nerves worse. Once the lady was done hooking up my mic, I inhaled a deep breath and exhaled it, sliding my hands along my pants legs to straighten them up. Robin Kinnis' wardrobe team gave me a lime green pantsuit to wear with a cream-colored turtleneck. I walked over to the vanity and looked into the mirror. There were so many different emotions going on inside of me and it showed on my face. I did the only thing I knew how to do to calm my nerves; I prayed.

"Thank you, God," I said in my head, "for allowing me to wake up. Thank You for even giving me this opportunity. God, I understand that I had to go through these trials and tribulations, so You could move in areas that I needed. That incident changed my life and is changing other people's lives. God, when I speak today, I ask that You move and speak through me. I just want to touch somebody out there and let them know Your presence is within me. God, I want somebody to be inspired to be a changemaker." I picked my head up and opened my eyes.

By time I was done with my prayer, a lady with a headset and clipboard charged towards me. "Faith, please follow me. You're on in five," she stated.

As I followed in the lady's footsteps, it was like my mind was going in slow motion. Flashbacks replayed in my head, but this time, I smiled. I was no longer held captive by my thoughts. Before I knew it, Robin Kinnis was announcing my name and it was time for me to walk out. Walking across the stage, I smiled and threw my hands up in the air, waving to the cheering crowd. Ms. Kinnis' set was nicely decorated. I sat down on the blue velvet couch beside her. I was so overwhelmed from the love I was receiving from the beautiful people in her audience. I truly needed this, and God knew that.

"Hello, sweetie," said Ms. Kinnis. "It's nice to finally meet you. You look amazing! I'm loving the green with your skin. It looks great. Thank you for coming!"

"Thank you for having me. It's my pleasure," I replied.

"Well, how are you adjusting to things? Your life must have truly flipped around since the bullying incident you dealt with at school."

I took a deep breath before answering the question, making sure I had comprehended every word. "Well, Ms. Kinnis, I'm going to be completely honest. When it first happened, I was in shock. I suppressed any pain immediately and everything went smoothly. Recently, though, I finally was able to deal with the situation," I said. "I felt like God was allowing me to deal with that situation, so I could level up. I was trying to move on without Him healing those wounds" Before I could even finish what I was saying, the crowd started with the *Oohs!* and *Ahs!* then when I was done, they burst into applause.

"I don't regret what I went through because somebody's life was changed in a positive way by it. God used me to make a change. Although I was humiliated, He knew He wouldn't have been able to use me without it. Now, I'm feeling much better today. I get positive messages on my page, in my text messages, and people post nice things to me all day long, so that really keeps me going."

Amya Meekins

"That's good," Ms. Kinnis said. "Your Mom did an excellent job raising you. You're so wise beyond your years. This generation needs you."

"Thank you, Ms. Kinnis," I said earnestly.

"So, you've created this campaign, Melanin Matters. I have to say; I absolutely love the idea of this. Colorism is such an important topic that is constantly overlooked. I think you're a very brave young lady. What are some of your plans for the campaign?"

"Well, Ms. Kinnis, I want the youth to grow up knowing that their skin tone is beautiful, no matter what society says. They belong, their melanin matters, and their future matters. I want to be able to help others find their purpose through God, so they can help others in the way that I was able to find my own. It's very important that we live the purpose God has for us. One day, I was scrolling down Instagram and saw this quote by Will Smith. It read, 'If you're not making someone else's life better, then you're wasting your time. Your life will become better by making others' lives better.' That made me look at life from a much more different perspective. My Grandma once told me that we must stop being 'self-focused' and become 'Christ-focused.' That hit the nail on the head for me.

"We're so used to how society wants us to be and the stereotypes that they've placed on us. None of that matters in God's eyes. We're going to be whoever He has called us to be and no man can stop that at all. I pray to God every day that He uses me to help impact my community, but in His way, and how He wants me to do it. I know there are other young people across the country who feel the exact same way as I do. Generation Z is something so special, and I know it. We just must realize our worth and use that for greatness. Uplift one another; break the barriers and the stereotypes society has placed over us. It seems like the system wants to see us fail as African Americans. So, Melanin Matters is to help kids discover their history, learn the roots of colorism, and empower excellence across the world."

"Y'all, I'm so blown away by this phenomenal young lady. Faith, you are incredible. You're going to go so far in life. Please keep being a leader. Thank you so much for coming on this show. It was so nice meeting you," Ms. Kinnis said.

"Wait," I interrupted. "Before I leave, Ms. Kinnis, I have a little surprise for you as a token of appreciation for giving me this opportunity."

"A surprise for me? I'm usually the one gifting people things on this show, not receiving." The lady who directed me onto the stage came out with the little gift bag I had brought.

"Here's a gift to show my appreciation," I said, handing her the bag. "Aww, thank you, sweetheart. This is so kind!" Ms. Kinnis gushed.

When she peeked inside the bag, she let out a small chuckle, definitely impressed. She pulled out her customized "Melanin Matters" t-shirt with her mouth in an "O" shape. The audience applauded and I hoped she was happy with her gift.

"Thank you so much," Ms. Kinnis said. "I can't wait to rock this." She gave me a big hug. "Make sure you guys go get your Melanin Matters merch. And we'll be back after break," Ms. Kinnis said to the cameras. Her smile was huge as she did her signature dance until the camera stopped rolling.

"That wasn't so bad," I sighed.

"Faith, I really appreciate this. You don't know the half of it. I'm always giving away things to people. You did what you did without looking to receive, so in return, I'm going to give you $20,000 for your Melanin Matters campaign. I believe in you. You're so wise and brilliant. You will be blessed."

Chapter Ten:

I was sitting on the balcony of our new penthouse apartment in downtown Westrock. The sun beamed on me as I drank my orange juice and ate some pancakes, sausage, and eggs for breakfast. It felt like God was smiling at me, like He was proud of me and thrilled that I had followed His path. My favorite tunes were blasting out of the speaker, making the mood even better. I was writing down some thoughts, happy to finally have some time to myself, when I heard a little knock. I turned around to see who it was, and a smile appeared on my face. Trevor walked in with a bouquet of flowers and some chocolate-covered strawberries. Why must this boy increase the level of "crush" I have for him?

"Hey, Faith, just wanted to stop by and give you a little gift in honor of your new accomplishments," he said, "but I see you're eating already. Oops!" He set the flowers on the table next to me and gave me a hug. He smelled so good as always.

Amya Meekins

"Sit! Let's open up these strawberries and chat!" I said, giggling. "So, Trevor, how have things been? I mean, like, you've just been evolving in life. You're so successful, and I'm so proud of you," I said, picking up a strawberry and biting into it.

"Thank you, Faith. I needed to hear that. My emotions have been all over the place and what you said just brought me peace. I'm proud of you too. You're so amazing. You literally took your pain and turned it into power. That's mad inspiring." He looked in my eyes. My heartbeat sped up as Trevor leaned in closer to me.

This would be my first official kiss. I was jumping up and down inside, having a whole dance party. Yes, I had a little kiss in elementary school —who hadn't? —, but this would count for sure. I don't care what anyone says, your first kiss doesn't count until you're old enough. Luckily, this one would be with the person I'd had a crush on for the longest. Nobody could tell me a thing.

I leaned into him too. As soon as our lips connected, I felt fireworks inside. I'd never felt like that before at all. Once we broke apart, we looked into each other's eyes. I knew Trevor felt the same vibe as me.

"Look at you, girl" he chuckled, but leaned back in for another one.

Just before our lips could touch again, his phone vibrated, killing the moment. He glanced to see who it was and sucked his teeth, shoving his phone back into his pocket. I could tell he was annoyed but wanted to create the vibe that was lost again. He moved towards me again, but his phone set off vibrating again. He checked the name but didn't ignore it this time. He picked up his phone and walked to the other side of the balcony. He was clearly frustrated, and I had a strange feeling myself. Something was wrong, I felt it in my gut. Suddenly, I got a text message that made me drop my phone: **Watch your back.**

I picked my phone up but was still shook. That text message was sent from an anonymous number. I looked around, checking my surroundings. *Who could this be and what did they mean? What did I do wrong? I asked myself.* I didn't want to tell Trevor and get him started. He had just come back into town and was trying to lay low with the "gang" stuff. I knew that if Trevor and Zay found out, these streets would be crazy for the next two weeks. Trevor hung up the phone and came back over to me.

"Um, Trevor, I have to tell you something," I said. My leg was shaking, but it wasn't to much for him to notice.

Amya Meekins

"My bad, that was the homie. What's up?" he asked but avoided my eyes. I knew from the past that when Trevor looked a certain way, he was doing something he didn't have any business doing.

"Trevor!" I hollered to get his attention and looked at him sideways.

"Yes?" he asked, finally looking up at me. It wasn't the same as when he looked in my eyes before kissing me. This time, he was guarded. "What's up?" I asked him. "Your vibe has been off ever since you received that phone call."

"Nothing," he replied. "I actually came over here to tell you I'm about to roll out." Suddenly, he stood and walked towards the balcony doors. I slumped down in my chair, disappointed. "Wait, didn't you say you had something to tell me? What's good?" he asked, turning around to face me.

"Oh, nothing," I said. "Love you, kid. Be safe. "

"Love you too!" he said. I really didn't want him to leave, but I got up to walk him out. "Where are you going, mama?" Trevor asked when I stood.

"I'm going to let you out," I said, locking the screen door to the balcony and walking over to open the front door.

Something wasn't right. We took the elevator down to the lobby, and my heart literally felt like it was dropping. My stomach felt a rush of butterflies. My hand shook uncontrollably. I tried to stop it, but I couldn't. At that point, I was trying to shake whatever feeling there was off of me. Why wouldn't it go away? Trevor was too busy scrolling on his phone to even notice. He seemed more chill now that he was leaving.

The elevator dinged and the doors opened. Trevor walked off first, and I followed him. The horrible feeling in my stomach got ten times worse now that we were out of the elevator. We walked out of the lobby and into the city. Surprisingly, it wasn't that busy. The sun was setting. No lie, it did feel good to spend today with Trevor, chilling on the balcony just vibing.

"Well, mama, I'm about to go. I'll call you when I get home," he said, clicking the key fob to unlock his luxury car.

"Alright, see you later" I said and turned, about to walk back into the building.

"Ah ah, where you going? Where my hug at? Don't get beat up now," he joked. I opened my arms and hugged him. Trevor gave the best hugs, and it was cute because I was so small compared to him. When we pulled apart, he grabbed a piece of my hair and placed it behind my ear. He rested his arms on my shoulders and smiled. Then, he kissed me on my forehead. I felt so protected and secure.

"I love you," he said.

At first, I didn't even see the black SUV speeding down the street. The window was rolled down, and there was a group of people with black masks on. I opened my mouth to scream, but no sound came out. Trevor hadn't even turned around before the first shots were fired.

Pow!

His body jerked in my arms and blood shot from his leg.

Pow!

That one went straight to his back. I looked into Trevor's eyes and could see the fear. He was scared, and I was too. This time, he dropped to the ground. The SUV sped off, but before they were gone, a familiar voice yelled, "I told you watch your back." They skirted off laughing out of the window. At the time, I was too overwhelmed to think about who it was though.

The scream I let out was ear-splitting. Trevor held onto me. I applied as much pressure as I could on his wounds. I had learned that from watching movies. I just kept yelling and applying pressure. Trevor was breathing slowly, and I couldn't tell if I was doing the right thing. I wanted to go get help, but I couldn't leave him. Trevor's eyes rolled to the back of his head, but I could tell he was still fighting. I was so focused on Trevor that I didn't even realize a lady behind me had called 9-1-1. I could hear the ambulance sirens approaching.

When the paramedics arrived, they rushed over to Trevor, pushing me out of the way. I saw blue gloves all over his body. They ripped his shirt open and began to work on him before lifting him up onto the stretcher.

"Excuse me?" a man was saying. I was so focused on Trevor; I wasn't sure how long he had been trying to get my attention.

"Yes," I answered him, surprised I could find words.

"Did you see what happened?" the man asked. "Do you know this young man?"

I feebly answered the man's questions and was relieved when he agreed to let me ride in the ambulance with Trevor. I climbed into the back of the ambulance and stared at him. My eyes moved down to his leg. I remembered he was also shot in his back. I thought whoever did this was trying to kill or paralyze him.

Trevor tried to reach for me but didn't have enough strength. I grabbed his hand and held it. As we were riding, I prayed. The machines started going crazy. His body started

Amya Meekins

to jerk. I prayed to God. I didn't want to lose the love of my life when things had just started to go so well for us.

About the Author

Amya Meekins is not a stranger to the arts. She is a teen musical artist, CEO, and motivational speaker. Amya has been writing songs, blogs, and speeches for several years now. Amya is a scholar who excelled and will be graduating a year early.

Made in the
USA
Middletown, DE